Mog's
Amazing Birthday Caper

Judith Kerr

COLLINS
PICTURE LIONS

For Tom, Tacy and Matthew

William Collins Sons & Co Ltd
London · Glasgow · Sydney · Auckland
Toronto · Johannesburg

First published in Great Britain by William Collins Sons & Co. Ltd in 1986
First published in Picture Lions in 1989

Picture Lions is an imprint of the Children's Division,
part of the Collins Publishing Group,
8 Grafton Street, London W1X 3LA.

Copyright in the text and illustrations © Kerr-Kneale Productions Ltd 1989

Printed by Warners of Bourne and London.

Aa

Mog accidentally ate an alligator
and all were amazed at the . . .

...BANG!

Bb

Boohoo!

"You clumsy cat!   You crushed the cake and candles!"

Mog creeps off . . .

Cc

crossly . . .   to a corner . . .   for a catnap.

D d

She dreams and dreams and dreams.
She dreams of dragons doing damage in the dark . . .

E e

. . . and elephants eating Emily . . .

Ff

. . . and her family floating far into a fog.

G g   Goodness!   A giraffe in the garden.

Hh

Mog
hisses
and
he
hops
into
a
helicopter.

Ii

"May I invite you to an ice cream?"
inquires an Indian.

Jj

A jaguar joins them with a jug of jelly . . .

K k

. . . to eat with a kipper and
ketchup from the kettle.

L l

But look who is lurking!
Lying low!   Licking lips!   It's . . .

N n

"Don't nip my nose, you nightmare nibbler!"

It has not noticed Nicky with his net.

Oo

Oh!   Ooh!   Oops!

Outwitted!

Outraged!

Overpowered!

Pp

Mog purrs, and they paddle past palm trees and parrots to a pale pink palace with purple pillars.

Qq

But what is that queer quiver?
A quake!   An earthquake!
"I feel quite queasy,"
says the queen.

R r

The raging river rises round them.
"Run!" she roars.　　"My royal rug will rescue us."

S s

Soaring into the sky, Mog sees survivors struggling on a sinking sofa, surrounded by smiling sharks.

T t

They're terrified!
They're Mr and Mrs Thomas!
They teeter, totter, trip,
their treacherous transport tilts . . .

Underwater Underwater

Uu

Unbalanced!

Upset!

Upended!

Underwater

V v

But on the verge of vanishing for ever,
Mog hears a voice,
first vague, then very vivid . . .

"Why are your whiskers wet?
What is this water?
Wake up!   We're on our way
to somewhere wonderful!"

W w

X x

Mog goes on an extremely

She examines an axolotl . . .

exciting expedition.

and exclaims at an ox.

She yawns at a yak,
and then – yippee!   Yummy! . . .

Z z

Out of the zigzag zip-bag zooms something to guzzle,

and to dazzle and to puzzle the zebras at the zoo.